THE FLYING PATCHWORK QUILT

THE FLYING PATCHWORK QUILT

By Barbara Brenner
WITH ILLUSTRATIONS BY FRED BRENNER

NEW YORK: YOUNG SCOTT BOOKS

IF it weren't for my mother, it would never have happened.

You see, my mother collects things. She goes to antique shops and she goes to auctions, and she buys old stuff and puts it around the house.

Well, one day my mother came home with an old pine chest. "It will be a perfect place to store winter clothes," she told my father. "And look what's at the bottom of it," she added.

"What is it?" asked my father. (He doesn't like old stuff the way my mother does.)

"It's a piece of an old patchwork quilt," Mother said. "Isn't it pretty?"

She held it up, and we all came around to take a
look. I had never seen anything like that patchwork quilt. It was small—only about as big as a
beach towel. And it was old—some of the threads
were barely holding together. But bright! It was

just about the most rainbow-colored thing I'd ever seen. It had been made by sewing bits of cloth patches together in a sort of star pattern. Some of it was yellow and some of it was red. Some was purple and pink and green. Some of the patches were checked, and some were striped, and other pieces were flowered.

"It is pretty," my father admitted, "but what are you going to do with it?"

"It'll come in handy," my mother said. That's what my mother always says when she doesn't know what to do with one of her old things.

She folded it carefully and put it away in the bottom of the chest.

That was the last I saw of the patchwork quilt for a long time. It lay at the bottom of the old pine chest, and when spring came it got covered with moth flakes and snowpants and winter hats and sweaters. Then one day . . .

My sister was the
one who made it
happen. My sister Ellen
is a lot younger
than I am—
she's only five.
She's always going
through a stage.
At that time she was
going through the stage
where she wanted to fly.
She was always trying. She
tried to do it all different
ways.

She pinned a towel
on herself like
Superman.
She made herself a
pair of paper wings.
She tried everything.
No matter how many
times I said it couldn't
be done, she went
on trying.
She held on to
an umbrella and
jumped off the
porch.

Well, one day we were out in the back yard. My mother came out. "Carl," she said to me, "I have to do a little shopping. Will you keep an eye on Ellen?"

"Sure," I said, "Don't worry about a thing." So my mother drove away.

I was busy building a rabbit hutch in a corner of the yard. I really kept more of an *ear* on Ellen than an eye on her, because she talks to herself. I figured that as long as I could hear her talking, she was O.K.

She started to play her flying game. She started

to jump off the doghouse roof. I could tell without looking that she was jumping off the doghouse roof. There were these thumping sounds of her hitting the ground. I looked over once or twice. Once I saw her standing on the doghouse with a balloon tied around her. I remember the balloon said "George's Barber Shop" on it. I watched her jump and land smack on the balloon, which broke with a loud POP. She picked herself up, brushed off her knees, and untied the string.

I felt a little sorry for her. "Ellen," I called to her, "it won't work. Why don't you give up?"

She looked at me stubbornly. "It will so work. I just haven't found the right flying thing yet. You'll see." And with that, she stomped off into the house.

I sighed and went back to my rabbit hutch.

A few minutes later I looked up and . . . "Oh, no," I groaned. There was Ellen, about to try flying with the old patchwork quilt! "No, you don't," I warned. "That belongs to Mother."

"Please, Carl. Just this once. I'll put it right back. I just want to *try* it."

I should never have let her. But she begged and begged, and so I finally said, "All right, but promise that after you fall down with the silly thing you will stop playing this game for the rest of the afternoon!"

She promised.

I helped her pin it on around her neck with a big safety pin. I gave her a hand up onto the doghouse again. Then I stood back so she could make her jump.

"One—two—three," she yelled.

"Jump," said I.

She did.

Now—I'm not making this up. One minute she was jumping off the doghouse roof. The next minute—there she was. Floating over my head. There she was. With her sneakers dangling in my face. There she was. Giggling and gliding all over the place. FLYING!

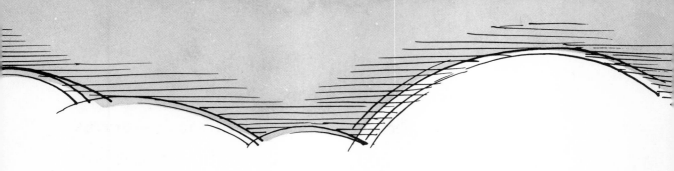

"I told you, I told you!" she kept hollering, as she flapped above my head. "I knew the patch-work quilt was the right thing."

I just stood there with my mouth open.

A breeze came along and tossed her up a little higher. She began to look a bit scared.

"Carl?" she called, kind of funny. I grabbed for her leg and missed.

The breeze got stronger. She went higher. And then higher and—right over the chimney. And before I knew it, the wind was blowing her over the housetops straight toward Nyack.

"Don't worry. I'm coming," I shouted, as I ran to the garage for my bike. By the time I started down the driveway, she was just a tiny speck in the distance. I pedaled furiously—across Wheeler Place and then down the Sickeltown Road hill, craning my neck for a glimpse of that crazy quilt and my little sister.

Soon I was at the Four Corners. But there

wasn't a sign of her.   Everything was just the way it always is at the Four Corners.

There was the Clarksville Inn.

There was Ted's Strawtown Grocery, with the specials of the day pasted on the window.

There was Marshall's Drugstore.   Mr. Marshall

was sitting outside as usual, sunning himself next to the newspapers. I skidded up to him.

"Mr. Marshall, Mr. Marshall," I panted. "Did you see my sister fly by just now?"

"In an airplane or on a flying carpet?" He chuckled.

I was in no mood for jokes. "As a matter of fact," said I, "it was a patchwork quil—Oh, never mind," I said miserably.

"Sorry, Carl, haven't seen her," said Mr. Marshall. "But if she lands on my roof, I'll let you know," he called after me.

I coasted down the hill toward Old Mill Road, trying to steer my bike and look up in the sky at the same time. I was getting a terrible crick in my neck. And I didn't seem to be any closer to finding Ellen and the flying quilt.

I was almost at Cassebeer's Flower Farm when I thought I spotted something. There seemed to be

a blob of orange drifting above the irises. I rode over there as fast as I could.

When I got to Cassebeer's, the orange thing was gone. All I could see were iris beds. You see, the Cassebeers plant iris like some farmers plant corn. Row on row of them. It was pretty hard to tell from the road whether there was a patchwork quilt with a girl attached to it among all those flowers.

So I left my bike and began to run up and down the rows. Past all the little signs with the names of the irises on them. *White Sprite* and *Orange Parade*. *Bermuda Sea* and *Mustard Pot*. *Greenspot*

and *Tinkerbell*. All the names I used to love to read to Ellen.

The iris beds run right down to the shore of Lake DeForest. As I came to the last clump, I looked out over the water.

There she was!

She was doing something that looked like water skiing without water skis. Her sneakers were getting awfully wet, and she looked plenty scared. Too scared even to yell. I waved frantically to Mrs. Cassebeer, who was digging in a clump of iris at the other end of the field. She just smiled and nodded and waved back. (Mrs. Cassebeer is very nearsighted.)

Did you ever have one of those dreams where you yell for help and no one hears you? That's how I felt. But then I looked at Ellen getting soaking wet, and I realized it was no dream. I had to get her away from the water. She can't even swim.

"Try to steer," I called to her. "Wrap the quilt around your arms. Flap your left arm and you'll go to the right. Flap your right arm and you'll go to the left."

"Which is left?" she called back.

I groaned. "Flap them both."

She did. Slowly she began to move away from the water.

As soon as she was over dry land, the wind took her higher again. I could not get close enough to grab her before she was gone, flying south like some bird taking off for the winter. The last thing I heard her say was something about wanting a

tuna fish sandwich and a chocolate milk-shake.

I climbed back on my bike again, and headed south. Past the brook. Past the old church and the cemetery. Past the library. As I whizzed by, I looked skyward.

And there was Ellen. Right smack on top of the library flagpole, hanging by the seat of her pants! Boy, was I glad to see her!

"Don't worry," I yelled, "help is on the way."

I ran into the library.

"Mrs. Lojahn," I shouted, shattering the quiet of the library.

Mrs. Lojahn, the librarian, hurried over, her finger against her lips.

"Shhhhhhhhhhhhhhhhhhhh."

"But, Mrs. Lojahn," (whispering) "my sister is outside on the flagpole, and. . ."

"Well, tell her to get off, dear, we don't like children to climb on the flagpole."

"You don't understand!" (Shouting.)

"Shhhhhhhhhhhhhhhhhhhh."

"I can't help it," (whispering) "my sister is in terrible danger."

"Whatever are you talking about, Carl?"

"My sister has been flying all over West Nyack, and now she's caught on top of the flagpole."

"WHAAAAAT!" cried Mrs. Lojahn, forgetting to whisper. Then she stopped herself. "Carl," she said sternly, "is this fact or fiction?"

I looked her straight in the eye. "It's fact, Ma'am. And please hurry, because if her pants tear. . ."

We hurried out of the library, Mrs. Lojahn and I. We ran down the library steps and into the yard. Shading her eyes, Mrs. Lojahn looked up to the top of the flagpole. I looked up too.

There was nothing there.

I looked at Mrs. Lojahn, and she looked at me. No use even trying to explain to her. I just turned away, got on my bike, and rode off. It's a good thing boys my age don't cry.

Well, let's face it, I said to myself, you have lost your sister, and nobody can help you because nobody will believe you. I thought about going to the Clarkstown Police and trying to make them understand. I thought about saying to them, "You see, my sister has flown away. She was wearing this patchwork quilt, and. . ." I shuddered at the thought.

Might as well go home. I walked my bike back up the long hill. My legs were aching. I had a terrible pain in my neck. And I wasn't looking forward to explaining everything to my mother.

When I rode into the driveway, my mother's car was there. I went in to break the news.

My mother was in the kitchen, fixing supper,

just as if there hadn't been a catastrophe. I walked into the kitchen.

"Mother," I said to her, "there has been a catastrophe."

"A what?" said my mother, turning around. "Where?"

"Right here. But it wasn't my fault."

"I'm sure it wasn't," said my mother, looking worried. "But tell me all about it."

"It's Ellen," I said, my mouth dry and my heart thumping.

"Yes, I meant to speak to you about that," my mother said. "Didn't I tell you to keep an eye on her? When I came home, you were gone."

"I tried to watch her, but she was too hard to follow," I said desperately.

Mom smiled. How could she, at a time like this?

"Now, come on, Carl. She's probably been sitting up in that apple tree ever since I left."

"What tree? Where?" I gasped.

Mother pointed. I ran to the window. I could hardly believe my eyes, but sure enough. There was Ellen, sitting in the apple tree at the far end of the yard, talking to herself a mile a minute.

I ran past my mother out into the yard. I climbed up next to Ellen, trying to keep myself from doing something foolish like *kissing* her.

"Where have you been?" I hissed, acting real mad.

"I couldn't help it, Carl," she said. "The patchwork quilt *made* me do it. I tried to turn. And I tried to go lower. I just couldn't. It was ever so scary. But it was great fun, too," she added. "And then I kept wishing that I could get home, and then I remembered what you said about flapping, and I flapped my arms real hard, and all of a sudden I was here. And now I'm caught on this tree and I can't get the quilt off and I don't want to tear it because Mom will be mad and—will you help me down, Carl?—Carl?"

I was only half-listening. Now that she was safe, I had begun to think about what had happened that morning. That strange, wonderful,

crazy quilt. A person could *fly* with that quilt
on!

I thought about pinning the quilt on myself.
I thought about flying to visit my grandmother in
Newark, New Jersey, or my uncle in Phoenix,
Arizona. I thought about flying to New York

City over the George Washington Bridge. Do you have to pay a toll if you go *over* the Bridge? I wondered.

I sat there in that old apple tree, just dreaming about flying around with the patchwork quilt.

Of course, I said to myself, you'll have to learn how to steer the thing.

Of course, I answered myself, I'll start right away. Right after school tomorrow.

My flying dreams were interrupted by my sister, who kept saying, "Please help me to get down. I'm caught and I don't want to tear the quilt."

I looked behind her. Sure enough, Ellen was all tangled in the quilt, and the quilt was all tangled in the tree. I decided to unpin Ellen first. While I was unpinning her, I talked—fast.

"Now, remember, not a word about this to Mom. She doesn't even know we have the quilt.

I'll smuggle it into the house and put it back in the chest. Quick. Scoot now." Down she went, and ran into the house.

I untangled the quilt and hid it inside my shirt so my mother wouldn't see it. As soon as I got into the house I raced upstairs. I was just about to

put the quilt back in the pine chest when the thought struck me. Why wait? Why not take a ride that very night?

So instead of putting the quilt safely back in the chest, I took it into my room.

That night I could hardly wait for everyone to go to bed. Ellen was asleep early, but my mother and father sat on the front porch for a long time. Finally, I heard my mother say, "Let's go in, dear, it's getting breezy." And then I heard the screen door close.

Everything was set for the take-off. My plan was to climb out on the roof and launch from there. The quilt was ready on the window sill. I slipped a jacket on and stuffed an apple into my pocket in case I got hungry. Quietly, I opened the window. A rush of cool air blew into the room. It *was* getting breezy!

I stood there for a minute, looking up into the

dark night sky. There was a moon; that would help. I picked up the quilt and slung it around my shoulders. "Well—here goes!" I muttered. Then—shucks! What happened to the safety pin? I put the quilt down and turned to get another pin from my dresser.

In that moment it happened. The wind
caught the quilt and blew it over the sill and out
the window. I made a wild grab for it, but too
late. As I watched in horror, it slid across the roof
and off the edge. The breeze lifted it and it
began to climb. Higher and higher. In two
minutes it was out of sight. Gone. Vanished.

And we never saw the patchwork quilt again.

I'd think I dreamed it all if it weren't for my sister, Ellen. She remembers everything. My mother remembers too, in a way. Every once in a while she says, "I wonder what became of that pretty little quilt that was in the pine chest?"

Then my sister gives me that look as if to say, "Why don't we tell them?"

But I shake my head. Nobody would believe us.

Ellen's out of her flying stage now. But I still have a scientific interest in flying. For instance, my mother came back from an auction the other day with an old hooked rug. It looked just like an ordinary rug. But—it may have possibilities. If someone were to take that rug to a fairly high place, say, oh—the top of a doghouse, and if someone were to sit in the middle of it, and then push off . . . well—who knows?

THE END

About the Author and Artist

The Flying Patchwork Quilt is Barbara Brenner's eighth book for children. She has also written book and lyrics for a children's musical, and has one adult nonfiction book to her credit.

Fred Brenner is well known as a fashion artist as well as an illustrator of children's books. He is an instructor at Parsons School of Design, where he teaches creative figure drawing and conducts an art seminar.

The Brenners live in West Nyack, New York, and *The Flying Patchwork Quilt* is liberally sprinkled with references to neighbors and scenes from this historic old town. The Brenner boys, Mark and Carl, admit that they both went through flying stages, and that some of their experiences found their way into the book.

This is Fred and Barbara Brenner's second book as a team. Their first, *A Bird in the Family,* was a Junior Literary Guild selection.